To Ben Brown with love from MMC

Text copyright © 2005 by Sally Grindley
Illustrations copyright © 2005 by Margaret Chamberlain

First published in the United States of America in 2006 by
Walker Publishing Company, Inc.
Distributed to the trade by Holtzbrinck Publishers

First published in the U.K. in 2005 by Bloomsbury Publishing Plc.

For information about permission to reproduce selections from
this book, write to Permissions, Walker & Company,
104 Fifth Avenue, New York, New York 10011.

Library of Congress Cataloging-in-Publication Data

Grindley, Sally.
It's my school / Sally Grindley ; illustrations by Margaret Chamberlain.
p. cm.
Summary: Tom is not happy that his younger sister, Alice, is starting kindergarten at his school.
ISBN-10: 0-8027-8086-5 • ISBN-13: 978-0-8027-8086-7 (hardcover)
ISBN-10: 0-8027-8087-3 • ISBN-13: 978-0-8027-8087-4 (reinforced)
[1. First day of school—Fiction. 2. Brothers and sisters—Fiction. 3. Schools—Fiction.]
I. Title: It is my school. II. Chamberlain, Margaret, ill. III. Title.
PZ7.G88446Its 2006   [E]—dc22   2005037181

Book design by Sarah Hodder

Visit Walker & Company's Web site at www.walkeryoungreaders.com

Printed in China

2 4 6 8 10 9 7 5 3 1

All papers used by Walker & Company are natural, recyclable products made from wood grown in well-managed forests. The manufacturing processes conform to the environmental regulations of the country of origin.

It's *My* School

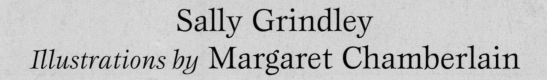

Sally Grindley

Illustrations by Margaret Chamberlain

WALKER & COMPANY · NEW YORK

It's your big day tomorrow," said Dad.
Alice hid under the covers.
    "Don't worry," said Dad. "Tom will look after you."

In his bedroom, Tom kicked his school shoes
lying on the floor and threw himself on the bed.
Why did his sister always have to spoil everything?

Dad came in and sat next to him.
"It won't be as bad as you think," said Dad.
Tom wriggled uncomfortably and turned away.
"I hope you'll be nice," said Dad.

In the morning, Alice stood by the front door, clutching her teddy bear.

"You can't take that stupid thing," snarled Tom. "Everyone will laugh at you."

In the car, Alice said excitedly, "Teddy's coming with me because he'll be lonely at home."

"Tom took Hoppit the Frog when he was your age," said Dad. "He wouldn't part with it."

When they stopped outside the school, Dad put an arm around Tom and said, "Please keep an eye on Alice. It's a big day for her."

"It's a *horrible* day for me," cried Tom, and he ran away.

"Will Tom play with me?" asked Alice as Dad took her to meet her teacher.

"I think you'll want to play with your new friends," said Dad.

"I don't think Tom likes me," said Alice.

Tom sat in his classroom and looked out the window. A line of kindergartners waddled across the playground. He looked for Alice. Her blond curls bobbed up and down in the middle of the line.

"Which one's your sister?" whispered a friend.

"Who cares?" hissed Tom, and he went back to his reading.

At lunchtime, Alice came rushing over to Tom and his friends. "Teddy likes it here," she said. "He wants to come again tomorrow."

Tom went bright red.

"You and your stupid teddy bear," he growled.

Alice's eyes filled with tears.

At recess, Tom kicked a ball and played tag
with his friends. But he couldn't help looking
around to see what Alice was doing.

Then he heard a loud cry.

"Tommy!"

Tom sprinted across the playground
and saw a boy holding his sister's teddy
bear. "I think that belongs to Alice," he
said. "Can I give it back to her?"
The little boy nodded.

Alice wiped her tears away and hugged her teddy bear tightly. Then Tom gave her a great big kiss, right on her cheek, and ran away.

Dad picked them up after school. But before he could ask how the big day had gone, Alice jumped into his arms and cried, "Tommy gave me a great big kiss, didn't you, Tommy?"

Tom growled and threw himself into the car, but a smile tugged at the corners of his mouth.